Louise Imogen Guiney

Songs at the Start

Louise Imogen Guiney

Songs at the Start

ISBN/EAN: 9783744767415

Printed in Europe, USA, Canada, Australia, Japan

Cover: Foto ©Andreas Hilbeck / pixelio.de

More available books at **www.hansebooks.com**

SONGS AT THE START

BY

LOUISE IMOGEN GUINEY

"And we sail on, away, afar,
Without a course, without a star,
But by the instinct of sweet music driven."
SHELLEY: *Prometheus Unbound.*

BOSTON

CUPPLES, UPHAM AND COMPANY

1884

C. J. PETERS AND SON,
STEREOTYPERS AND ELECTROTYPERS,
145 HIGH STREET.

ERRATA.

PAGE 10. Third line : read *haunt* for *haunts*.

PAGE 26. Tenth and eleventh lines : omit the word *no*.

THIS

FIRST SLIGHT OUTCOME OF TASTES TRANSMITTED BY
MY FATHER,

Is Enscribed to His Friend and Mine,

JOHN BOYLE O'REILLY.

CONTENTS.

Songs at the Start.

Songs at the Start.

GLOUCESTER HARBOR.

North from the beautiful islands,
North from the headlands and highlands,
    The long sea-wall,
The white ships flee with the swallow;
The day-beams follow and follow,
    Glitter and fall.

The brown ruddy children that fear not,
Lean over the quay, and they hear not
    Warnings of lips;
For their hearts go a-sailing, a-sailing,
Out from the wharves and the wailing
    After the ships.

Nothing to them is the golden
Curve of the sands, or the olden
      Haunts of the town ;
Little they reck of the peaceful
Chiming of bells, or the easeful
      Sport on the down :

The orchards no longer are cherished;
The charm of the meadow has perished :
      Dearer, ay me !
The solitude vast, unbefriended,
The magical voice and the splendid
      Fierce will of the sea.

Beyond them, by ridges and narrows
The silver prows speed like the arrows
      Sudden and fair ;
Like the hoofs of Al Borak the wondrous,
Lost in the blue and the thund'rous
      Depths of the air ;

On to the central Atlantic,
Where passionate, hurrying, frantic
     Elements meet ;
To the play and the calm and commotion
Of the treacherous, glorious ocean,
     Cruel and sweet.

In the hearts of the children forever
She fashions their growing endeavor,
     The pitiless sea ;
Their sires in her caverns she stayeth,
The spirits that love her she slayeth,
     And laughs in her glee.

Woe, woe, for the old fascination !
The women make deep lamentation
     In starts and in slips ;
Here always is hope unavailing,
Here always the dreamers are sailing
     After the ships !

LEONORE.

You scarce can mark her flying feet
  Or bear her eyelids' flash a space;
Her passing by is like the sweet
  Blown odor of some tropic place;
She has a voice, a smile sincere,
The blitheness of the nascent year,
  April's growth and grace;
All youth, all force, all fire and stress
In her impassioned gentleness,
Half exhortation, half caress.

A thing of peace and of delight, —
  A fountain sparkling in the sun,
Reflecting heavenly shapes by night, —
  Her moods thro' ordered beauty run.

Light be the storm that she must know,
And branches greener after snow
   For hope to build upon ;
Late may the tear of memory start,
And Love, who is her counterpart,
Be tender with that lily-heart !

A BALLAD OF METZ.

Léon went to the wars,
　True soul without a stain;
First at the trumpet-call,
　Thy son, Lorraine!

Never a mighty host
　Thrilled so with one desire;
Never a past Crusade
　Lit nobler fire.

And he, among the rest,
　Smote foemen in the van,—
No braver blood than his
　Since time began.

And mild and fond was he,
　And sensitive as a leaf;—

Just Heaven! that he was this,
  Is half my grief!

We followed where the last
  Detachment led away,
At Metz, an evil-starred
  And bitter day.

Some of us had been hurt
  In the first hot assault,
Yet wills were slackened not,
  Nor feet at fault.

We hurried on to the front;
  Our banners were soiled and rent;
Grim riflemen, gallants all,
  Our captain sent.

A Prussian lay by a tree
  Rigid as ice, and pale,
And sheltered out of the reach
  Of battle-hail.

His cheek was hollow and white,
　Parched was his purpled lip;
Tho' bullets had fastened on
　Their leaden grip,

Tho' ever he gasped and called,
　Called faintly from the rear,
What of it?　And all in scorn
　I closed mine ear.

The very colors he wore,
　They burnt and bruised my sight;
The greater his anguish, so
　Was my delight.　　　　　　•

We laughed a savage laugh,
　Who loved our land too well,
Giving its enemies hate
　Unspeakable:

But Léon, kind heart, poor heart,
　Clutched me around the arm;

"He faints for water!" he said,
   "It were no harm

To soothe a wounded man
   Already on death's rack."
He seized his brimming gourd,
   And hurried back.

The foeman grasped it quick
   With wild eyes, 'neath whose lid
A coiled and viper-like look
   Glittered and hid.

He raised his shattered frame
   Up from the grassy ground,
And drank with the loud, mad haste
   Of a thirsty hound.

Léon knelt by his side,
   One hand beneath his head;
Not kinder the water than
   The words he said.

He rose and left him so,
   Stretched on the grassy plot,
The viper-like flame in his eyes
   Alas! forgot.

Léon with easy gait
   Strode on; he bared his hair,
Swinging his army cap,
   Humming an air.

Just as he neared the troops,
   Over there by the stream —
Good God! a sudden snap
   And a lurid gleam.

I wrenched my bandaged arm
   With the horror of the start:
Léon was low at my feet,
   Shot thro' the heart.

Do you think an angel told
   Whose hands the deed had done?

To the Prussian we dashed back,
  Mute, every one.

Do you think we stopped to curse,
  Or wailing feebly, stood ?
Do you think we spared who shed
  A friend's sweet blood ?

Ha ! vengeance on the fiend :
  We smote him as if hired ;
I most of them, and more
  When they had tired.

I saw the deep eye lose
  Its dastard, steely blue :
I saw the trait'rous breast
  Pierced thro' and thro'.

His musket, smoking yet,
  Unhanded, lay beside ;
Three times three thousand deaths
  That Prussian died.

And he, my brother, Léon,
  Lies, too, upon the plain:
O teach no more Christ's mercy,
  Thy sons, Lorraine!

[This incident actually befell a private in a Massachusetts volunteer regiment, belonging to the Fifth Corps, at the battle of Malvern Hill.]

PRIVATE THEATRICALS.

You were a haughty beauty, Polly,
    (That was in the play,)
I was the lover melancholy ;
    (That was in the play.)
And when your fan and you receded,
And all my passion lay unheeded,
If still with tenderer words I pleaded,
    That was in the play !

I met my rival at the gateway,
    (That was in the play,)
And so we fought a duel straightway ;
    (That was in the play.)
But when Jack hurt my arm unduly,
And you rushed over, softened newly,
And kissed me, Polly ! truly, truly,
    Was that in the play ?

DIVINATION BY AN EASTER LILY.

Out of the Lenten gloom it springs,
　　Out of the wintry land,
White victor-flower with breath of myrrh,
Joy's oracle and harbinger;
　　I take it in my hand,

I fold it to my lips, and know
　　That death is overpast,
That blessèd is thy glad release,
And thou with Christ art full of peace,
　　Dear heart in Heaven! at last.

THE RIVAL SINGERS.

Two marvellous singers of old had the city of
    Florence, —
She that is loadstar of pilgrims, Florence the
    beautiful, —
Who sang but thro' bitterest envy their exquisite
    music,
Each for o'ercoming the other, as fierce as the
    seraphs
At the dread battle pre-mundane, together down-
    wrestling.
And once when the younger, surpassing the best
    at a festival,
Thrilled the impetuous people, O singing so
    rarely !
That up on their shoulders they raised him, and
    carried him straightway

Over the threshold, 'mid ringing of belfries and
    shouting,
Till into his pale cheek mounted a color like
    morning
(For he was Saxon in blood) that made more
    resplendent
The gold of his hair for an aureole round and
    above him,
Seeing which, called his adorers aloud, thanking
    Heaven
That sent down an angel to sing for them, taking
    their homage ; —
While this came to pass in the city, one marked
    it, and harbored
A purpose which followed endlessly on, like his
    shadow.
Therefore at night, as a vine that aye clambering
    stealthily
Slips by the stones to an opening, came the
    assassin,
And left the deep sleeper by moonlight, the
    Saxon hair dabbled

With red, and the brave voice smitten to death
    in his bosom.

Now this was the end of the hate and the striv-
    ing and singing.

But the Italian thro' Florence, his city familiar,

Fared happily ever, none knowing the crime and
    the passion,

Winning honor and guerdon in peaceful and
    prosperous decades,

Supreme over all, and rejoiced with the cheers
    and the clanging.

Carissima! what? and you wonder the world
    did not loathe him?

Child, he lived long, and was lauded, and died
    very famous.

AFTER THE STORM.

I.

Now that the wind is tamed and broken,
  And day gleams over the lea,
Row, row, for the one you love
  Was out on the raging sea:
    Row, row, row,
Sturdy and brave o'er the treacherous wave,
  Hope like a beacon before,
    Row, sailor, row
Out to the sea from the shore!

II.

O ño, the oar that was once so merry,
O ño, but the mournful oar!
Row, row; God steady your arm
To the dark and desolate shore:

Row, row, row,
With your own love dead, and her wet gold head
Laid there at last on your knee,
Row, sailor, row,
Back to the shore from the sea !

HEMLOCK RIVER.

On that river, where their will is,
Grow the tranquil-hearted lilies ;
In and out, with summer cadence,
Brown o'erbrimming waters slide ;

Shade is there and mossy quiet, —
O but go thou never nigh it !
Ghosts of three unhappy maidens
Float upon its bosom wide.

ON ONE POET REFUSING HOMAGE TO ANOTHER.

A NAME all read and many rue
Chanced on the idle talk of two ;
I saw the listener doubt and falter
Till came the rash reproof anew.

Then on his breath arose a sigh,
And in the flashes of reply
I saw the great indignant shower
Surcharge the azure of his eye.

Said he : "'Neath our accord intense
At mutual shrines of soul and sense,
Flows, like a subterraneous river,
This last and only difference.

"Behold, I am with anguish torn
   That you should name his name in scorn,
   And use it as an April flower
   Plucked from his grave and falsely worn :

"Thrice better his renown were not !
   And he in silence lay forgot,
   Than to exhale a strife unending
   Should be his gentle memory's lot.

"How can you, freedom in your reach,
   Nurse your high thought on others' speech,
   And follow after brawling critics
   Reiterating blame with each ?

"The world's ill judgments roll and roll
   Nor touch that shy, evasive soul,
   Whose every tangled hour of living
   God draws to issues fair and whole.

"It grieves me less that, purely good,
   His aims are darkly understood,

Than that your spirit jars unkindly
Against its golden brotherhood.

" *Et tu, Brute !* Where he hath flown
On kindred wing you cross the zone,
And yet for hate, thro' lack of knowing,
Austerely misconstrue your own.

" No closer wave and wave at sea
Than he and you for grace should be ;
I would endure the chains of bondage
That you might share this truth with me !

" A leaf's light strength should break the wind,
Ere my desire, your wilful mind ;
If I should waste my lips in pleading,
Or drain my heart, you still were blind,

" Still warring on the citadels
Of Truth remotely, till her bells
Rouse me, your friend, to old defiance, —
Tho' dear you be in all things else, —

" And tho' my hope the day-star is
  Of broadening eternities,
  Wherein, the shadows cleared forever,
  Your cordial hand shall rest in his."

BROTHER BARTHOLOMEW.

BROTHER BARTHOLOMEW, working-time,
 Would fall into musing and drop his tools;
Brother Bartholomew cared for rhyme
 More than for theses of the schools;
And sighed, and took up his burden so,
Vowed to the Muses, for weal or woe.

At matins he sat, the book on his knees,
 But his thoughts were wandering far away;
And chanted the evening litanies
 Watching the roseate skies grow gray,
Watching the brightening starry host
Flame like the tongues at Pentecost.

" A foolish dreamer, and nothing more;
 The idlest fellow a cell could hold; "

So murmured the worthy Isidor,
　　Prior of ancient Nithiswold;
Yet pitiful, with dispraise content,
Signed never the culprit's banishment.

Meanwhile Bartholomew went his way
　　And patiently wrote in his sunny cell;
His pen fast travelled from day to day;
　　His books were covered, the walls as well.
"But O for the monk that I miss, instead
Of this listless rhymer!" the Prior said.

Bartholomew dying, as mortals must,
　　Not unbelov'd of the cowlèd throng,
Thereafter, they took from the dark and dust
　　Of shelves and of corners, many a song
That cried loud, loud to the farthest day,
How a bard had arisen, — and passed away.

Wonderful verses! fair and fine,
　　Rich in the old Greek loveliness;

The seer-like vision, half divine ;
  Pathos and merriment in excess.
And every perfect stanza told
Of love and of labor manifold.

The King came out and stood beside
  Bartholomew's taper-lighted bier,
And turning to his lords, he sighed :
  " How worn and wearied doth he appear, —
Our noble poet, — now he is dead ! "
"O tireless worker ! " the Prior said.

RESERVE.

You that are dear, O you above the rest!
Forgive him his evasive moods and cold;
The absence that belied him oft of old,
The war upon sad speech, the desperate jest,
And pity's wildest gush but half-confessed,
Forgive him! Let your gentle memories hold
Some written word once tender and once bold,
Or service done shamefacedly at best,
Whereby to judge him. All his days he spent,
Like one who with an angel wrestled well,
O'ermastering Love with show of light disdain;
And whatsoe'er your spirits underwent,
He, wounded for you, worked no miracle
To make his heart's allegiance wholly plain.

PATRIOT CHORUS ON THE EVE OF WAR.

In thy holy need, our country,
Shatter other idols straightway ;
Quench our household fires before us,
Reap the pomp of harvests low ;
Strike aside each glad ambition
Born of youth and golden leisure,
Leave us only to remember
Faith we swore thee long ago !

All the passionate sweep of heart-strings,
Thirst and famine, din of battle,
All the wild despair and sorrow
. That were ever or shall be,
Are too little, are too worthless,
Laid along thine upward pathway

As with our souls' strength we lay them,
Stepping-stones, O Love! for thee.

If we be thy burden-bearers,
Let us ease thee of thy sorrow;
If our hands be thine avengers,
Life or death, they shall not fail;
If thy heart be just and tender,
Wrong us not with hesitation:
Take us, trust us, lead us, love us,
Till the eternal Truth prevail!

LO AND LU.

WHEN we began this never-ended
 Kind companionship,
Childish greetings lit the splendid
 Laughter at the lip ;
You were ten and I eleven ;
 Henceforth, as we knew,
Was all the mischief under heaven
 Set down to Lo and Lu.

Long we fought and cooed together,
 Held an equal reign,
Snowballs could we fire and gather,
 Twine a clover chain ;
Sing in G an A flat chorus
 'Mid the tuneful crew, —

No harmonious angels o'er us
    Taught us, Lo or Lu.

Pleasant studious times have seen us
    Arm-in-arm of yore,
Learnèd books, well-thumbed between us,
    Spread along the floor;
Perched in pine-tops, sunk in barley,
    Rogues, where rogues were few,
Right or wrong, in deed and parley,
    Comrades, Lo and Lu.

Which could leap where banks were wider,
    Mock the cat-bird's call?
Which preside and pop the cider
    At a festival?
Who became the finer Stoic
    Stabbing trouble thro',
Thrilled to hear of things heroic
    Oftener, Lo or Lu?

Earliest, blithest! then and ever
  Mirror of my heart!
Grow we old and wise and clever
  Now, so far apart ;
Still as tender as a mother's
  Floats our prayer for two ;
Neither yet can spare the other's
  "God bless — Lo and Lu!"

HER VOICE.

A LARK from cloud to cloud along
In wildest labyrinths of song, —
So jubilant and proud and strong;

A ray that climbs the garden wall
And leaps the height at evenfall, —
So clear, so faint, so mystical;

A summer fragrance on the breeze,
A shower upon the lilied leas,
A sunburst over violet seas,

A wand of light, a fairy spell
Beyond a faltering lip to tell;
Bright Music's perfect miracle.

Still live the gift outrunning praise,
Inviolate from this earthly place
And fitly pure for heavenly days,

Sincerity its stay and guard,
A glowing nature, happy-starred,
Its dwelling now and afterward!

Where'er that gentle heart shall be,
Responsive to their source I see
The fount and form of melody;

And my foreshadowed spirit drawn
Of hindrance free, and unforlorn,
To list thro' some ambrosial dawn,

To follow with oblivious eyes
The old delight, the fresh surprise,
Adown the glades of Paradise!

AN EPITAPH.

FUGITIVE to nobler air,
Dead avow thee who shall dare?
Freeborn spirit, eagle heart,
Full of life thou wert and art!
Tender was thy glance, and bland;
Honor swayed thy giving hand;
Sweet as fragrance on the sense
Stole thy rich intelligence,
And thy coming, like the spring,
Moved the saddest lips to sing.

Wealth above all argosies!
Sunshine of our drooping eyes!
Be to Heaven, for Heaven's desert,
Fair as unto us thou wert.

Tho' the groping breezes moan
Here about thy burial-stone,
Never sorrow's lightest breath
Links thy happy name with death,
Lest therein our love should be,
Thou that livest! false to thee.

THE FALCON AND THE LILY.

My darling rides across the sand;
The wind is warm, the wind is bland;
It lifts the pony's glossy mane,
So light and proud she holds his rein.
Not easier bears a leaf the dew
Than she her scarf and kirtle blue,
And on her wrist, in bells and jess,
The falcon perched for idleness.
That merry bird, O would I were!
In joy with her, in joy with her.

My darling comes not from her bower,
The lowered pennon sweeps the tower;
The larches droop their tassels low,
And bells are marshalled to and fro.

My heart, my heart, beholds her now,
The pallid hands, the saintly brow,
The lily with chill death oppressed
Against the summer of her breast :
That lily pale, O would I were !
In peace with her, in peace with her.

BOSTON, FROM THE BRIDGE.

THIS night my heart's world-roaming dreams are
    met,
The while I gaze across the river-brim,
Beyond the anchored ships with cordage dim,
To the clear lights, that like a coronet
On thee, my noble city, nobly set,
Along thy summits trail their golden rim.
Peril forsake thee! so shall peal my hymn;
Glory betide thee! Nor may men forget,
Shelter of scholars, poets, artisans!
The sap that filled the perfect vein of Greece,
And hung with bloom her fair, illustrious tree,
Unheeded, thro' dull eras made advance,
Unfruitful, stole to topmost boughs in peace
Twice centuries twelve; and flowered again in
    thee.

THE RED AND YELLOW LEAF.

THE red and yellow leaf
Came down upon the wind,
Across the ripened grain ;
The red and yellow leaf,
Before me and behind,
Sang shrilly in my brain :

" Pride and growth of spring,
Ease, and olden cheer,
Shall no longer be :
What benighted thing,
Dreamer, dost thou here ?
Follow, follow me !

" Youth is done, and skill ;
What is any trust

Any more to thee ?
Pale thou art and chill ;
All of love is dust :
Follow, follow me ! "

" Thou red and yellow leaf,
O whither ? " from my staff
·I called adown the wind ;
The red and yellow leaf,
I heard its mocking laugh
Before me and behind !

"POETE MY MAISTER CHAUCER." *

SOMEWHERE, sometime, I walked a field wherein
The daisies held high festival in white,
Thinking: Alas! he with a young delight
Among them once his golden web did spin;
He who made half-divine an olden inn,
The Tabard; sung of Ariadne bright,
And penned of Sarra's king at fall of night,
"Where now I leave, there will I fresh begin."
Then straightway heard I merry laughter rise
From one that wrote, thrown on a daisy-bed,
Who, seeing the two-fold wonder in mine eyes,
Spake, lifting up his fair and reverend head:
"Child! this is the earth-completing Paradise,
And thou, that strayest here, art centuries dead."

* Lydgate so calls him,
. . . . "of righte and equitie,
Since he in Englishe in rhyming was the beste."

MOUNT AUBURN IN MAY.

THIS is earth's liberty-day:
Yonder the linden-trees sway
   To music of winds from the west,
And I hear the old merry refrain,
Of the stream that has broken its chain
   By the gates of the City of Rest,

The City whose exquisite towers
I see thro' the sunny long hours
   If but from my window I lean;
Yea, dearest! thy threshold of stone,
Thine ivy-grown door and my own
   Have naught save the river between.

Thine on that heavenly height
Are beauty, and warmth, and delight;
   And long as our parting shall be,
Live there in thy summer! nor know
How near lie the frost and the snow
   On hearts that are breaking for thee.

AMONG THE FLAGS

IN DORIC HALL, MASSACHUSETTS STATE HOUSE.

DEAR witnesses, all luminous, eloquent,
Stacked thickly on the tesselated floor!
The soldier-blood stirs in me, as of yore
In sire and grandsire who to battle went :
I seem to know the shaded valley tent,
The armed and bearded men, the thrill of war,
Horses that prance to hear the cannon roar,
Shrill bugle-calls, and camp-fire merriment.
And as fair symbols of heroic things,
Not void of tears mine eyes must e'en behold
These banners lovelier as the deeper marred :
A panegyric never writ for kings
On every tarnished staff and tattered fold ;
And by them, tranquil spirits standing guard.

CHILD AND FLOWER.

*[From the French of Chateaubriand.]**

ALONG her coffin-lid the spotless roses rest
   A father's sad, sad hand culled from a happy
      bower ;
Earth, they were born of thee : take back upon
    thy breast
      Young child and tender flower.

To this unhallowed world, ah! let them not re-
    turn,
    To this dark world where grief and sin and
     anguish lower ;
The winds might wound and break, the sun might
    parch and burn
      Young child and tender flower.

* The author's title runs: "Sur la Fille de mon Ami, enterrée
devant moi hier au Cimetière de Passy: 16 Juin, 1832."

Thou sleepest, O Elise! thy years were brief and
    bright;
  The burden and the heat are spared thy
    noonday hour;
For dewy morn has flown, and on its pinions
    light,
    Young child and tender flower.

KNIGHT FALSTAFF.

I saw the dusty curtain, ages old,
Its purple tatters twitched aside, and lo!
The fourth King Harry's reign in lusty show
Behind, its deeds in living file outrolled
Of peace and war; some sage, some mad, and
  bold:
Last, near a tree, a bridled neighing row
With latest spoils encumbered, saints do know,
By Hal and Hal's boon cronies; on the wold
Laughter of prince and commons; there and here
Travellers fleeing; drunken thieves that sang;
Wild bells; a tavern's echoing jolly shout;
Signals along the highway, full of cheer;
A gate that closed with not incautious clang,
When that sweet rogue, bad Jack! came lumber-
  ing out.

THE POET.*

LISTEN! the mother
Croons o'er her darling;
Birds to the summer
Call from the trees;
Sailors in chorus
Chant of the ocean:
The poet's heart singeth
Songs sweeter than these.

Thy lute, gentle lover,
To her thou adorest;
Ye troubadours! pæans
For princes of Guelph:

* For this trifle, obligations are due to Maestro Mozart. A sunny
little opening Andante of his, from the Second Sonata in A major, sug-
gested immediately and quite irresistibly the words here appended,
which follow its rhythm throughout.

But Heaven's own harpers
Breathe not in their music
The song that his happy heart
   Sings to itself;
The changeless, soft song that it
   Sings to itself!

A CRIMINAL. 1865.

"CLOSE as a mask he wore this fiery sin
Of hate ; and daring peril foremost, died
Ere yet the wrath of law was justified,
Hopeless, with memory such as miscreants win.
One sacred head he smote, encircled in
A people's arms ; and shook, with storms allied,
The pillars of the world from side to side." ...
E'en so the Angel's record must begin.
Show me not anguish since that traitor-stroke
Rang o'er the brunt of war ; yet child, O child !
When later days bring bitter thoughts, recall,
No maledictions on his name I spoke,
Catching lost cues ; but asked, well-reconciled,
God, our Interpreter, to right us all.

ORIENT–BORN.

BEAUTIFUL olive-brown brows, chin where the
    fairy-print lies ;
Vagrant dark tresses above splendid mysterious
    eyes ;

Mellowest fires that glow under the calm of her
    face,
Girl of all girls in the world for mould and for
    color and grace.

Such are the opal-like maids that flash in the
    groves to and fro,
Dancers Arabian ; such, languorous ages ago,

Ptolemy's daughter; and so, breathing faint
    cassia and musk,
Veilèd young Moors on divans, singing and
    sighing at dusk.

Never in opiate dreams have I o'ertaken you,
    sweet ;
Never with henna-tipped hands ; never with
    silken-shod feet ;

Still the love-charm of the East must over and
    over be told :
By-and-by havoc with hearts ! . . . Ah, slowly,
    my seven-year-old !

CHARONDAS.

He lifted his forehead, and stood at his height,
  And gathered the cloak round his noble age,
This man, the law-giver, Charondas the Greek ;
And loud the Eubœans called to him : " Speak,
  We listen and learn, O sage ! "

" In peace shall ye come where the people be,"
  Spake the lofty figure with flashing eyes :
" But whoso comes armed to the public hall
Shall suffer his death before us all."
  And the hearers believed him wise.

The years sped quick and the years dragged
      slow ;
  In council oft was the throng arrayed,

But never the statued chamber saw
The gleam of a weapon; for loving the law,
  The Greeks from their hearts obeyed.

War's challenge knocked at the city gates;
  Students flocked to the front, grown bold;
The strong men, girded, faced up to the north;
The women wept to the gods; and forth
  Went the brave of the days of old.

Peace winged her flight to the city gates;
  Young men and strong, they followed fast
Back to the breast of their fair, free land:
Charondas, afar on the foreign strand,
  Remained at his post the last.

Their leader he, in war as in word,
  The fire of youth for his life-long lease,
The strength of Mars in the arm that stood
Seven hot decades upheld for good
  In the turbulent courts of Greece.

The fight is finished, the council meets.
   Who is the tardy comer without
In cuirass and shield, and with clanking sword,
Who strides up the aisles without a word,
   Rousing that awe-struck shout?

The tardy comer home from the field —
   Great gods! the first to forget and belie
The law he honored, the law he formed:
" Charondas — stand! you enter armed,"
   With a shudder the hundreds cry.

The men who loved him on every side,
   The men he led to the victor's gain,
He paused a moment, the fearless Greek;
A sudden glow on his ashen cheek,
   A sudden thought in his brain.

" I seal the law with my soul and might:
   I do not break it," Charondas said.
He raised his blade, and plunged to the hilt.
Ah! vain their rush, for in glory and guilt.
   He lay on the marble, dead.

CRAZY MARGARET.

THAT is she across the way,
Dressed as for a holiday,
Wandering aimlessly along
In oblivion of the throng,
With her lay of old regret ;
That is crazy Margaret.

And her tale floats up and down
This enchanted Norman town,
Told among the wharves and ships,
On the children's babbling lips,
Over gossips' window-sills,
In the rectory, thro' the mills.

Very sad and very brief,
Graven on a cypress leaf,
Is the record of her days.
When the aloes were ablaze
Long ago, in summertide,
He maid Margaret cherished, died.

Hush! there is the holier part :
He knew nothing of her heart.
Tears thrilled in her lustrous eye
But to see him passing by,
And she turned from many a claim
Dreaming on that dearest name.

Solely on his thoughts intent
The rapt student came and went,
All the gladness in his looks
Sprung from visions and from books,
Grave with all, and kind to her,
His meek peasant worshipper.

So she loved him to the last,
Keeping her soul's secret fast,
Suffering much and speaking naught
Of the woe her loving wrought;
Till the second summertide,
The young stranger drooped and died.

At the grave, before them all,
In the market, in the hall,
Down the forest-paths alone,
Ever since, in undertone
She goes singing soft and slow:
"When I meet him, he shall know."

Therefore is she eager yet,
Poor, unhappy Margaret,
Holding still, in faith and truth,
The lost idyl of her youth,
Seeking fondly and thro' tears,
One who sleeps these forty years.

Should he haunt our Norman coast,
Should he come, the gentle ghost ;
Should she tell him of her pain,
Of her passion hushed and vain, —
Would he grieve ? or would he care ?
What a tragic chance is there !

TO THE WINDING CHARLES.

THOU wanderer, what longing hath
    Thee peace on earth denied,
Ah, tell me : constant in no path,
    Thy pensive currents glide.

From dim pursuit and mocking zest,
    Would I could set thee free !
My soul hath its divine unrest,
    Dear river, like to thee.

MY NEIGHBOR.*

WHO art thou that nigh to me
Alone dost dwell, perpetually?
The latch against thy door is mute,
I have not heard thy kind salute,
And though I live here at the gate,
Have never known thy birth or state,
Nor seen thy wide colonial lands
With slaves obeying all commands,
Or children playing at thy knee;
Ah, neighbor mine, unneighborly!

The sun beats hard upon thy roof,
The tree's cool shadow waves aloof;

* Jacob Sheafe, an old Boston worthy, laid away in 1658, in a quiet
northerly corner of King's Chapel Burying-Ground.

Thou dost not heed, nor speak in ire,
Nor wound thy calm with vain desire.
The cones that patter as they fall,
The drifts that build thine outer wall,
The rains that glisten in the trace
Of thine inscription, dimmed apace,
The winds that blow, the birds that sing, —
Thou carest not for any thing !

Two centuries and more art thou
In solitude abiding ; now
This town is other than thy town ;
Its lanes are highways broad and brown ;
The oaken houses of thy day,
And inns, and booths, are swept away.
Strange spires would meet thine eager eye,
New ships sail in, new banners fly ;
And names are kept of them that fell
In wars to thee incredible.

How beautiful thine endless rest !
The quiet conscience in thy breast,
Thy hidden place of peace, where pass
The ghost-like stirrings of the grass ;
The long immunity from strife,
The tumult, love ; the trouble, life ;
The blossom at thy feet, to be
A thousand summers, dust like thee ;
The winding-sheet, that white as worth,
Shuts all.thy failings in the earth.

My silent neighbor ! thou and I
Keep unobtrusive company.
For us each wild October weaves
The glistening clouds, the glowing leaves,
And March by March the robin sings,
Against the solemn porch of King's,
His sweet good-morrow to us both.
O be not harsh with me, nor wroth,
That I, apart from all the throng,
Break, too, thy silence with a song !

THE SEA-GULL.

OVER the ships that are anchored,
　　Over the fleets that part,
Over the cities dark by the shore,
　　High as a dream thou art!

Beautiful is thy coming,
　　Light is thy wing as it goes;
And O but to leap and follow this hour
　　Thy perfect flight to the close,

O but to leap and follow
　　Where freedom and rest may be;
Where the soul that I loved in surpassing love
　　Hath vanished away, with thee!

LILY–OF–THE–VALLEY.

Darling of the cloistered flowers,
Rising meekly after showers,
  Every cup a waving censer, —
Winds are softer at thy coming;
By thee goes the wild bee, humming
  Music richer and intenser.

Indian balsam is thy breathing,
Sabbath stillness thy enwreathing;
  Peace and thee no thought can sever.
In thy plaintive looks and tender,
Things of long-forgotten splendor
  Thrill my inmost spirit ever.

And I love thee in such fashion,
With so much of truth and passion,
  In this sad wish to enshrine thee:

Only pure hearts be thy wearers,
Only gentlest hands thy bearers,
  Even if therefore mine resign thee ;

Even if now I yield thee wholly
To the pure and gentle solely,
  On whose breast thy cheek is lying !
Droop and glisten where she laid thee,
And remember me that made thee,
  Dear, so happy in thy dying.

LOVER LOQUITUR.

LIEGE lady! believe me,
　　All night, from my pillow
I heard, but to grieve me,
　　The plash of the willow;
The rain on the towers,
　　The winds without number,
In the gloom of the hours,
　　And denial of slumber:

And nigh to the dawning, —
　　My heart aching blindly,
Unresting and mourning
　　That you were unkindly —
What did I ostensibly,
　　Ah, what under heaven,
Liege lady! but sensibly
　　Doze till eleven?

VITALITY.

When I was born and wheeled upon my way,
As fire in stars my ready life did glow,
And thrill me thro', and mount to lips and lids :
I was as dead when I died yesterday
As those mild shapes Egyptian, that we know
Since Memnon sang, are housed in pyramids.

TO THE RIVER.

FRIEND CHARLES! 'tis long since even for a space
We stood in cordial parley: you and I,
(Albeit about the selfsame city lie
The daily orbits we in silence pace), .
Seldom, how seldom, see each other's face!
Always had you a mill to turn near by,
A race to aid; and I, with scarce a sigh,
Passed, on like duties bound with heavy grace.
But now good Leisure puts all things in tune,
Now o'er their brimming bowls in odorous whiff
The gods send up the clouds above us curled,
Let us go forth, my Charles! thro' fields of June
Together, gladly, lovingly, as if
We could not have enough of this sweet world.

THE SECOND TIME THEY MET.

"Oh, would I might see my love," sang he,
  As he dreamed in his true heart of her,
As he rode that day up the highway wide,
With his feathers gay, and the lute at his side ;
"Oh, would I might see my love," sang he,
  "My love that knows not I love her."

"Oh, would I might see my love," sang she,
  As she sat in the porch above him,
With the web half-spun in her fingers fair,
And a ray of the sun in her brown, brown hair ;
"Oh, would I might see my love," sang she,
  "My love that knows not I love him."

Then as their eyes met, with a start I forget
    Whether shame, or delight, or sorrow,
The sky in its glow seemed to interest her,
And he bent very low to fasten his spur ;
But "Oh, would I might see my love,"—dear me!
    They sang it no more till the morrow.

ON NOT READING A POSTHUMOUS WORK.*

THEY stirred the carven agate door
Back from the cloisters, where of yore
One toiled by night, and toiling, kept
   The starlight on his bended head :
"O enter with us, straight and free,
The master's place of mystery ;
Had he not gone beyond the sea,
   He would have bid us come," they said.

But from the threshold hushed and gray
The loiterer turned, and made his way
From arch to arch, and answered low,
   Pale with some ever-deepening dread :

* Hawthorne's "Doctor Grimshawe."

" What he once promised to unfold,
Without him, how shall I behold ?
O enter you whose hearts are bold;
     My heart hath failed me here," he said.

Thou dead magician, be it so !
I close thy pages, and forego
The beauty other men may scan
     With much of awe and tenderness;
And if this blessing half-divine,
With gracious sorrow I resign
To faith that firmer is than mine,
     Thou knowest if I love thee less !

BESSY IN THE STORM.

"Why come ye in with tresses wild,
    With baffling winds aweary,
All damp and cold, my bonny girl,
    My deary?

" The sun not yet has oped his lids,
    The clouds hold fast together ;
Why stirred ye out this angry morn,
    And whither ?"

" O mother mine! mayhap I rose
    To fetch the gillyflower,
Or soothe my sister's little son
    An hour ;

" Or else I led a bleating lamb,
    Strayed off from any other,
Or went to pray at break of day,
    Sweet mother ! "

" My Bess, my lass, deceive me not ;
    So long it had not taken."
" O no ; O no ! I did for grief
    Awaken.

" My true love never you have seen,
    Down by the ships I found him ;
In all the gale, I held mine arms
    Around him.

" He spake to me, he kissed me thrice,
    And sailed the seas a-mourning ;
And then my tears rained with the rain
    Returning."

AFTER A DUEL.

"In fair and discreet manhood; that is, civilly, by the sword." — *Ben Jonson*.

By laurels upon your brow
  New-placed, our worth is reckoned :
You are a hero now,
  And I, — a dead man's second.

Your prowess was most fair,
  And fairer yet I own it ;
A majesty lies there,
  And you have overthrown it.

To dexterous hands was given
  Your weapon giant-hewing ;
The lightning out from heaven
  Had scarcely dared its doing !

For balm on wounds aghast
  Supreme in you my trust is;
Solicitous to the last,
  Your pity tempered justice.

Thanks, to my final breath,
  For challenge, thrust, and parry.
With this pale weight of death
  Your living praise I carry.

I see no hate abhorr'd,
  But courtesy acting thro' you:
' The Devil, sweet my lord,
  Be thus considerate to you!

In honor, after a lapse,
  Dare you to combat sprightly,
Thenceforth you chance mishaps
  To superintend, — politely.

INDIFFERENCE.

As once in a town thro' the twilight pleasant
  A belfry chorus majestic rose,
While our talk ran on, and the good lamp glis-
    tened,
And nothing you recked, rapt soul! but listened,
  And followed on truant wing incessant
    After the chime to its silvern close;

So later, when over your gentle pages,
  The harsh world wronged you with scorn and
    sting,
By the far-away joy in your blue eye growing,
I knew that beyond these ill winds blowing,
  You heard, my Poet! the praise of the ages;
    Only and ever you heard them sing.

THE PLEDGING.

"We buried a loving heart to-day;
We miss his coming over the way,
  The toss of his hair, his laughter's ring;

"The radiant presence gone from earth;
The serious eyes that could shine with mirth,
  The luminous brain, the hand of a king;

"So, losing him as we did, I say
Fill up the goblets, and glad and gay
  On his lonely road we will drink him cheer:

"Health to the fine old friend we knew!
Peace to his slumbers under the dew!
  Hail to his memory kind and dear!

" And for second pledge, fill up to the brim ;
(Laugh lightly, what if our eyes be dim !)
   Here's to the first that shall follow him."

The sun ran riot across the floor ;
Pomegranate-blossoms swung by the door ;
   Blithe robins lit on the ivied sill :

The voice in the gurgle of wine was lost ;
Up from the board were the beakers tossed ;
   Loud clashed their rims with a royal will.

And he, the youngest, that swayed them erst,
Poured yet again, like a man athirst :
   " To the first who follows we drink, we three ! "

Sudden beside him Another stood,
So sudden, he fell as the sandal-wood
   Sinks when the axe is laid to the tree :

But the Shadow lifted his cup instead
With the old quick smile, and the toss of the
     head :
   " Franz ! thou art the first to follow ! " he said.

AT GETTYSBURG.

BELLS of victory are dumb ;
Trailing sword and muffled drum
    On we come,

Downcast eyes and broken tread,
Weary arms, and burdenèd
    With our dead.

Lives were proffered : reck not his ;
For dear Freedom's ransom is
    Sacrifice.

Proud our love is, nor at last
With a sorrow that is past
    Overcast.

O'er the very clay we bring,
Meet it is that we should sing
     Triumphing :

He was foremost, he was leal ;
Let his gallant breast reveal
     Honor's seal.

Him we yield the Roman crown,
Woven bays ; in his renown
     Lay him down.

Earth will softest pillow make,
So that never heart shall ache
     For his sake ;

Spring will pass here many a day,
Sighing, one with thoughts that pray
     Far away,

"When the trumpets shake the sod,
Raise Thy Knight from this dull clod,
     Lord our God ! "

EARLY DEATH.

A YOUNG bird fell last night across the dark
And was not.   In the willow hung its nest ;
But yesterday, with proud and beating breast,
From bough to bough it crossed a fairy arc ;
Among its kindred barely did we hark
Its first delightful carol, or note the crest
Grow into golden-violet loveliest ;
There was no dial in our thought to mark
The sealèd possibilities of days,
The unwrought miracle of happy singing :
And now, tho' newly fail our earthly sense,
Elsewhere that delicate intelligence
Bursts into blossom of harmonious lays,
All summer on a comely tree-top swinging.

MY SOPRANO.

(II. L.)

Loving her, what should I fail to do for her?—
Keep season on season sunny and blue for her,
Lengthen her days like a happy tale,
With thoughts all tender and hearts all true for
    her,

Ward her from trouble, good tidings bring to
    her;
Fight for her, laugh with her, comfort her, cling
    to her,
But if I were even a nightingale,
I wonder — if I should dare to sing to her!

THE CROSS ROADS.

OUT from the prison at twilight,
With stealthy, terrible swiftness,
Darted one of the branded, life beating in every
vein ;
Freedom stirring his pulses,
Gladness and fear and longing
Surging thro' brain and body with precious
unwonted pain.

Out from the damp, dark cell,
The shackles, the sorrowful silence,
Out from the ring of faces and the jarring of
stern commands,
Forth to the scent of the meadows,
The glisten of garrulous brooklets,
And the dim, kindly evening he blessed with
his weary hands.

On, like the sweep of a scimitar
Dashed he, cutting the darkness,
Or as the storm blows on, none knowing its
way or its will ;
Cumbered with horrible fears,
Leaped he the perilous ledges
Reaching the village that lay in the valley,
untroubled and still.

Midway of his sickening haste,
Sudden he faltered and moaned,
Seeing three stand by a window, as the breeze
loitering blew ;
A woman sad-featured and patient,
Two golden heads at her shoulder,
Dear eyes he made shine once — dear childish
hair that he knew !

Not yet, for surely the bloodhounds
Would track him thither to-morrow ;
Not yet ! tho' soon that door should open, as
long ago :

Dashing the tear from his cheeks,
The bronze, rough cheeks that it hallowed,
He rushed on.   Had they seen it, the poor,
wan face ?   Did they know ?

Here meet the roads : see, eastways,
The long, clear track to the forest,
There, with chestnuts shaded, the path to the
inland town :
Behind, a glimpse of the village,
Front — four sharp cliffs to the ocean ;
Quickly, which shall he choose ?   Hark ! the
captors are hunting him down !

Shuffle of hurrying feet,
Breathings nearer and nearer.
No choice for a man that is doomed, unless
straight to the merciful sea.
Up to the toilsome cliffs !
Better death than new anguish !
A cry, a plunge . . . shine, stars, on the rip-
ples that ring that sea.

Soft in the ominous shadow the branches stir
    by the meadow,
Fair in the lonely distance the dying household
    glow ;
    Deep in the dust of the street,
    Just where the four roads meet,
Two trembling forms where he stood a moment
    so ;
    And a wistful child's voice said,
    Touched with great trouble and dread :
" O little sister ! which way did father go ? "

"HEART OF GOLD."

LADY serene, benign,
This dainty name of mine,
Pride in my bashful eyes
  Bending to see,
With your look eloquent,
Oft for glad service lent,
Laughingly, lovingly,
  Gave you to me.

Generous gift bestowed!
Lofty desert avowed!
Queen and true Knight indeed
  Played we those days;
All of my faith unspent,
Full of my child's content,
Shyly, yet haughtily,
  Wore I your praise.

O for that happy sport
Once in your mimic court!
O for your voice again,
    Lips silencèd!
O for the olden name
Ere disillusion came ;
O for "the golden heart,"
    Too, that is dead !

A JACOBITE REVIVAL.

ONE voice I heard of a ghostly horde,
About a visionary board,
      That said,
While goblets filled with ruby-red :
"Can you remember, good my lord,

"Among the newer creeds and laws,
The unrevived, pathetic cause
      Of kings ?
Can you remember all such things ?
How long, how long ago it was !

"What is the story ? Rivets loose,
Superb contrivance ; fainter use ;
      For years,
Allegiance, consecrate with tears,
Sad loyalty, its own excuse ;

"A morning faith magnificent;
Defiance breaking; ardor spent
      And pains
For royal blood thro' dwindled veins,
Half-clogged with dust of dull content,

"But weak not wholly; for there burst
In the last scion, battle-nursed,
      Such scope
Of rich emprise, that our rash hope
Wrote him not last, indeed, but first.

"For our true liege folk mocked at ease,
And chartered foes, and crossed the seas:
      Behold!
Where are they now, the gaps, the old
Delicious taunts and enmities?

"Then, troops of gallant gentlemen
That passed by night o'er field and fen,
      Did shout
Townward, lusty and loud throughout:
'When the King comes back to his own again.'

" Then rose a prayer, heart-tremulous,
Near many an heir, in many a house,
     Asleep:
' O kindly. Heaven ! do thou but keep
Our children rebels after us !'

" Then sailors landing from the fleet,
Idling wits in a sunny street,
     And sirs
With trim-clipp'd beards and rattling spurs
Met, swearing fealty : so we meet.

" And since the stars, and you, and I
Have seen the cycle rolling by,
     And know
That right is right, thro' flower and snow,
Why then, give still the wonted cry :—

" Here 's to the proud, forgotten names,
Here 's to the Stuart, Charles and James !
     Ah me !
Full few that live so long as we
Fan older love to steadier flames.

" Here 's to our fathers, Cavaliers ;
Their noble toil, their patient years
That bore
A burden precious now no more :
So may they rest in happier spheres.

" And here 's our benison for her
Who doth the forfeit sceptre stir ;
A toast
Late in the day, and welcome most :
Death and doom to Hanover ! "

   .   .   .   .

Now this I heard from comrades dead,
And vowed Amen to all they said,
And rose
With fair intent to draw more close ;
But like the forest deer they fled.

SPRING.

"With a difference." — HAMLET.

AGAIN the bloom, the northward flight,
The fount freed at its silver height,
And down the deep woods to the lowest,
The fragrant shadows scarred with light.

O inescapeable joy of spring!
For thee the world shall leap and sing;
But by her darkened door thou goest
Forever as a spectral thing.

ADVENTURERS.

WHEN we were children, at our will,
  That vanished summer blithe and free,
Dear shipmate! how we loved to float
Thro' wind and calm, in a little boat,
  All alone on the sparkling sea!

One morn, defying storms we sailed
  And sang our Credo, you and I —
"Beyond the foam, the surge, the mist,
The sea-fog's moving amethyst,
  The peaceful fairy islands lie."

And far we urged the forward prow,
  Half-mad with longing as we hied ;
Yet at the sunset's dying glow
Faint-hearted, ceased, and homewards so
  Came meekly with the evening tide.

Surely, the Isles of Rest were near !
  Why did our childish ardor tire ?
Now more, oh, more the thousandth time !
We thirst for that celestial clime,
  We hunger with that old desire.

Some day, when we shall sail again,
  The home-lights late indeed may burn ;
Let signals flutter on the shore,
Let tides creep up to the open door,
  But with no tide shall we return.

L'ETIQUETTE.

NEVER one in your kingdom, my queen,
Who stands in your presence serene,
Would take the first step less or more,
Or pose otherwise on the floor,
Or bend a whit deeper the knee,
Or speak but as low as can be,
And then at your royal command ;
And never a lord in the land
Would stir the fine blade in its sheath,
Or a marchioness rustle her wreath,
Or a page grow too lean or too stout
For fear of an exile, no doubt.
And yet I remember the first
Thro' order and system to burst,
Old freedom of ways to reclaim,
Was that blithe little fellow who came

To the arras majestic one day,
In his lace and his velvet array,
And rioted gallantly round,
And talked of his horse and his hound,
And gave milord's buckler a clang
And leaped o'er the marbles, and sang,
And laughed in barbarian glee,
Disturbing your stately levee ; —
Till the horrified ladies came down
And bore him away, at your frown.

That was a twelvemonth ago.
You sit there as placid as snow :
In ease and politeness and state,
The court holds its doings of late,
With nothing to vex with a qualm
That formal, respectable calm.
Patrician reproofs are forgot,
Since further ill-doers are not.

Liege lady ! say, what would you give
Henceforward as long as you live,
For the roguish soft clutch at your hair,
The capers and curvets in air,
The laughter's wild musical flow,
That you frowned at a twelvemonth ago?

THE GRAVE AND THE ROSE.

[Translated from Victor Hugo.]

WHISPERS the grave to the rose:
" With the dew that the dawn bestows,
What dost thou, love's darling blossom ? "
And the rose to the grave soft saith :
" And thou, dread abyss of death,
With them in thine awful bosom ? "
But answers : " Mystical tomb,
From the dew I exhale in the gloom
Mine odor of amber and spices."
Then the grave : " Ah, querulous flower !
Even so from each heart in my power
An angel to Heaven arises."